HELLO, STAR

Books by Carolyn Haywood

HELLO, STAR

HELLO, STAR

CAROLYN HAYWOOD

Illustrated by
JULIE DURRELL

Troll Associates

A TROLL BOOK, published by Troll Associates,
Mahwah, NJ 07430

Published by arrangement with William Morrow and Company, Inc.
For information address William Morrow and Company, Inc.,
105 Madison Avenue, New York, New York 10016.

First Troll Printing, 1988

Printed in the United States of America.

10 9 8 7 6 5 4 3 2 1

ISBN 0-8167-1310-3

★ ★

Dedicated with love
to
my ever helpful friends,
Glenna and Michael Liuzzi

★   ★

Contents

HELLO, STAR

★ 1 ★

Star and the Egg

Betsy had been six years old when Star was born. She was born on Christmas Eve, so Betsy was given the joy of naming the baby. She named her Star because she felt the baby should have a very Christmasy name. Sometimes Betsy called her Twinkle, "because," she said, "she's such a twinkly baby."

Now Star was five years old. This summer she was staying with her grandparents while Betsy was at summer camp and her father and mother were off on a long trip. Star called her grandparents "Grammy" and "Grampy." She loved playing with the animals on their farm.

Grammy had chickens. She had a lot of red ones and just one white one. Star loved the white

1

chicken and wanted it for a pet. She wanted to pick it up and carry it, but it was much too big for Star to carry.

When Star complained about not being able to pick up the chicken, Grammy said, "The little dog, Snowball, can be your pet."

"But I can't pick up Snowball," said Star.

"When you are bigger," said Grammy, "then you will be able to pick up both Snowball and the chicken."

"Oh, not both at once," said Star. "I couldn't carry Snowball and Chickie at the same time. They wouldn't like it. They wouldn't like it at all."

"No," said Grammy, "I didn't mean that you should pick them up at the same time. I just mean you'll be big enough to pick up Snowball and you'll be big enough to pick up Chickie."

The first morning at the farm, Star walked to the side of her grandmother's bed and said, "Time to get up."

Her grandmother, who was still sleeping, told her, "Oh, not yet, Star, the chickens aren't even awake yet."

Star went back to her little bed. As soon as she heard a rooster crow, she ran to her grandmother and said, "There's a chickie." Then her grandmother knew that it was time to get up.

Now Star listened for the rooster every morning, so that she would know when to wake her grandmother.

Star, being five years old, was able to dress herself and tie her shoes. Then she would run out to the hen house to get a freshly laid egg. The brown eggs were all right, but white eggs were her favorites. So when she reached the hen house, she looked through the nests until she found a white egg. She never knew whether Chickie had laid the egg, but if it was white, she was happy. She lifted the egg out of the nest and carried it with two hands to her grandmother to cook for her breakfast.

Star always watched while her grandmother scooped the egg out of the shell and dropped it into a cup with pieces of fresh bread. Then Star would clap her hands and laugh, saying, "It is turning yellow, Grammy. Good yellow egg. The chickens lay yellow eggs just for me."

One morning, as Star was carrying an egg, she tripped over a branch that had fallen on the path. Star didn't fall, but she dropped the egg.

"Whoops," she said, and looked down, but she didn't see a white egg on the ground anywhere. She looked in the flower bed, but she didn't see any white egg. She parted the leaves on the plants, but she didn't see any white egg.

Just then Snowball ran up the path, stopped, and looked up at Star. She patted her on the head and said, "Hello, Snowball, did you see my egg?"

Snowball licked her chops, and Star saw right away that there was yellow egg on the little dog's mouth. "Oh, Snowball," cried Star, "you ate my egg. You naughty girl. There won't be any egg for my breakfast."

Star went into the kitchen to her grandmother. "I dropped my egg, and Snowball ate it all up. Now there won't be any egg for my breakfast."

"Oh, yes, there will," said her grandmother as she picked up a brown egg. She was about to put it into the pan when Star cried out, "Grammy, I just like yellow eggs."

"There are no yellow eggs, Star," said her grandmother. "There are brown eggs and white eggs, but no yellow eggs."

"But I always have a yellow egg for breakfast," said Star. "And it turns the pieces of bread all yellow."

"Well, you just watch," said her grandmother as she emptied the soft egg out of the shell and dropped it into the cup. Then she broke bread into the cup, too.

Star looked down into the cup. As her grandmother stirred it around, Star watched the bread turn yellow. She cried out, "It's a good egg, just like always! Nice and yellow!"

Soon there was egg on Star's mouth, just as there had been on Snowball's.

★ 2 ★

The Swans

A road ran in front of Grammy and Grampy's house. Across the road and at the foot of a hill there was a pond with two beautiful white swans. The owner of the swans was a farmer who lived at the top of the hill.

A short way down the road from the pond there was a smaller house, where Star's Aunt Jessie, Uncle Jess, and seven-year-old cousin had come to spend the summer. Her cousin's name was Jeremy, but everyone called him Jerri.

Since he was born, Jerri had lived in England with his parents because his father worked there. But now they had come back to the United States and rented the little house to be near Grammy and Grampy for the summer.

When Jerri saw the swans, he said, "Oh, I know

all about swans. When we lived in England, the back of our house faced the river. There were a lot of swans swimming up and down on the river."

It wasn't long before Star began to think of Jerri as a big brother. He always took her hand when they crossed the road.

Both children loved the swans, but Star called them "swannies."

Star thought the large white birds were very beautiful. She said to her grandfather, "I would like the swannies for my pets."

And her grandfather said, "You mustn't think, because the swans are so beautiful, that they are friendly birds. They are not friendly, so you mustn't get too close to them."

"Maybe they would like somebody to be friendly," said Star.

"Well," said Grampy, "it's nice to be friendly, but you keep your friendship for the robins that peck on the lawn."

Star pointed across the road and said, "Is that bunch of straw the swannies' nest?"

"I suppose that's where it is," said her grandfather. "I don't know much about swans, but I guess they have nests just like other birds."

8

"They're the most beautiful birds I have ever seen," said Star. "And I love the swannies."

One morning, when Star's grandmother looked out the front window, she was surprised to see Star in the middle of the road. Grammy ran to the front door and opened it. "Star," she called out. "Come back! Come back at once!"

Star turned around and started to come back. But her grandmother ran to her and said, "Star, what are you doing out in the road?"

"I'm going to get the egg out of the swannies' nest," said Star. "Then you can cook it for my breakfast."

"There's no egg in the swans' nest," said her grandmother. "Swans don't lay eggs every day as the chickens do."

"Too bad," said Star. "No swannie eggs for my breakfast. Not ever?" she questioned.

"Not ever," said her grandmother.

One morning the following week, Jerri came to Star, who was sitting on the front step of the farmhouse.

Jerri was excited. "Oh, Star," he said, "the swans are nesting."

"How do you know?" asked Star.

"Well," replied Jerri, "my daddy was talking to Mr. Sawyer, that farmer who lives up on the hill. You know he owns the swans. He told my Daddy that there are beautiful eggs in the nest. The swans will take turns keeping them warm. And someday baby swans will come out of the eggs. Come on, Star, maybe we can see the eggs. But we won't get too close."

"I can't come," said Star. "Grammy won't let me go to see the swannies."

"Oh, I'll take your hand," said Jerri. "Come on!"

Star placed her hand in Jerri's, and they crossed the road. Before they reached the nest, the swans flew toward the children. When the children heard the swans hissing and honking, they began to run toward Jerri's house. Their legs flew as the swans rushed after them. The front steps of Jerri's house seemed farther away than ever before. But the children kept ahead of the swans until at last Jerri and Star scrambled up the steps.

The noise had awakened Snowball, who was having a nap on the porch. She jumped up, barking furiously, but did not go after the swans. The swans hissed at all of them angrily and then went back to the pond. Snowball, still barking, ran back

and forth in front of the house, while Star and Jerri sat huddled together trying to catch their breath.

Jerri's mother had heard all the noise. She came to Star and Jerri, who were trying to get over their fright.

"Star," said her Aunt Jessie, "did your grandmother know you were over near the swans?"

"It's my fault," said Jerri. "I wanted to show Star the swans' eggs that are in the nest."

"You must be very careful," said Star's aunt, "not to disturb the swans, especially when they are nesting on their eggs."

"Oh, Aunt Jessie," said Star, "will there be baby swannies?"

"Well, let's hope so," said her aunt. "Maybe in about a month we'll see some little ones swimming in the pond. The little ones are called 'cygnets.' "

"Oh!" said Star. "I can't wait to see those little cygnets. Are they like a signet ring? My daddy had a signet ring with his initials on it."

"No," said Aunt Jessie. "Baby cygnets and signet rings are entirely different. You'll find out when those eggs are hatched and you see the babies swimming around on the pond."

★ 3 ★

A Friendly Raccoon

Jerri was sitting on the back porch with his father and mother. Dinner was over, and it was now dusk. Jerri's pet lamb was nibbling the grass. Jerri's eyes were always on the lamb, whom he called "Beauty." So Jerri was surprised when his mother called out, "Well, look who's here!"

Jerri looked, and there, coming through the garden, was a raccoon. "Oh," he cried, "I hope he won't bother Beauty."

"I don't think he'll bother Beauty," said his mother. "But I must go inside and get some raisins for our visitor. Raccoons just love raisins."

Jerri's mother went into the kitchen and came back with a handful of raisins, which she spread over the bottom porch step.

"He's a cute thing," said Jerri.

"He's cute all right," said his father, "but he'd better keep away from the swans."

Jerri and his father and mother sat on the porch and watched the raccoon eat his raisins until it grew quite dark. "I wonder where that raccoon lives," said Jerri.

"Oh, down in the bushes somewhere," said his father.

"Jerri, it's time for you to go to bed," said his mother as she opened the screen door.

Sometime in the middle of the night, Star was awakened by screechings and wailings. They seemed to be under her window. Star jumped out of bed just as her grandfather came into her room.

"Oh, Grampy," cried Star, "what's that terrible noise?"

"Sounds like some animals," said her grandfather. "They seem to be in a big fight from the noise they are making."

Star's grandfather went to the window and opened the screen. Star joined her grandfather and stuck her head out the window. "What is it, Grampy?" she asked. "Is it the swannies that are making such a noise?"

"I think so!" said her grandfather. "I have a

feeling there's a raccoon out there."

"Oh, Grampy, a raccoon isn't after the swannies, is it?" asked Star.

Her grandfather laughed. "No," he said. "The swannies seem to be chasing the raccoon, and what a noise they are making doing it!"

"They're brave, aren't they," said Star.

"Indeed they are," said her grandfather.

"Oh," said Star, "wait until I see Jerri. I'll have a big story to tell him, won't I?"

"Indeed you will," said her grandfather as he tucked her back into bed.

The following morning, when Star saw Jerri, she said, "I saw the swannies being very brave last night. A raccoon was trying to pick a fight."

"How do you know?" said Jerri.

"Grampy and I saw it all out the window. And we saw the swannies chase the nasty raccoon."

"What do you mean, nasty raccoon!" exclaimed Jerri. "I guess that was the raccoon we saw at my house. We gave him raisins. He's a friend of mine. And I don't think it was nice of the swans to chase him."

"Well, he's a nasty raccoon," said Star. "He was trying to kill the swannies."

"Well, those swans are chasers," said Jerri.

16

"Didn't they try to chase us? And now they chased my friend the raccoon. I hope he will come back this evening for more raisins."

"If I come down to your house this evening, can I see the raccoon?" asked Star.

"Sure," said Jerri.

"You're sure he's a friendly raccoon?" Star asked. "And not a nasty raccoon?"

"Course he's not nasty," said Jerri. "He's my friend, and I don't have nasty friends."

"All right," said Star, "I'd like to meet him. What's his name?"

"He didn't tell me," said Jerri. "But I think George would be a nice name for him."

"George *is* a nice name," said Star. "But I don't think I can come to meet George because I'm not allowed to cross the road by myself."

"Oh, that's all right," said Jerri. "I'll come and get you. Didn't I take you across the road when we went to see the swans? I'm big now. I'm seven years old. When I go back to school in September, I'll be in the second grade. I can cross the road. Course, I have to look both ways before I do. You just trust me, Star."

"You're a nice boy, Jerri, and I'm glad you're my friend," said Star.

★ *4* ★

A Surprise

After supper, Jerri came to take Star over to his house to see the raccoon. Star was very excited as she held on to Jerri's hand.

"Jerri, you're *sure* this is a friendly raccoon?" asked Star.

"Oh, I'm sure," replied Jerri. "He's very friendly. Didn't he eat raisins that my mother put out for him?"

"Well, a big black bear would eat raisins, too," said Star. "But big black bears aren't friendly."

"Well, you just wait until you see him," said Jerri.

Jerri and Star joined his father and mother on the back porch. Jerri looked around and said, "The raccoon will come back, won't he?"

"It's a little early yet in the evening," said his mother. "I think he'll come back for more raisins."

"Oh, I hope so," said Jerri.

"I hope so, too," said Star. "I want to see him. Jerri says that his name is George and that he's friendly."

It wasn't long before there was a rustling noise just beyond the garden. Jerri said, "Listen. I think he's coming."

Star began to feel so excited. She felt tingly all over as she joined Jerri, who was leaning over the porch railing.

"I can see him coming," said Jerri as he pointed to the garden path. "Oh, my," Jerri cried out, "he's not alone. There's another raccoon with him."

"That's because of the raisins," said his mother. "Now, just look there. Why, he's brought his wife and the family. See, there are two little ones. I'll have to put out more raisins to feed this crowd."

Jerri's mother went into the kitchen and came back with a larger box of raisins. She spread the raisins on the step as she had done the night before. The raccoons lost no time in finding them.

Star's eyes were as big as saucers as she watched the raccoons picking up the raisins and putting

19

them in their mouths. "Oh, aren't those babies cute?" said Star. "I want to hold one in my lap."

"Star," said her Aunt Jessie, "you can't hold a raccoon in your lap. It's not a pussycat."

"But I want to hold it in my lap," said Star, beginning to cry.

"But these are not pets," said Jerri's mother.

Star continued to cry. "But Jerri said it was a friendly raccoon," she said. "Why did you say he was friendly, Jerri?"

" 'Cause he ate our raisins," said Jerri.

"Well, the babies are eating raisins," said Star. "Doesn't that mean they're friendly?"

"Oh, Star," said Jerri's mother, taking Star on her lap, "just enjoy watching them."

Now Star began to laugh, for one of the babies came so close to her that she was able to feed a raisin to it. "Look," said Star, "that baby wants to be a pet." But when she tried to pick it up, it ran to its mother.

Jerri's mother laughed. "See, Star, it's just a mama's baby."

"Well, I'm going to name it 'Kristy,' " said Star, "and the other one I'm going to name 'Josie.' "

"What shall we name the mother?" said Jerri.

"What about 'Mildred'?" said Jerri's father. "I have to put my two cents' worth into this show."

Jerri laughed. "I think George would like a wife named Mildred, but he would probably call her 'Millie.' "

At that moment, George opened his mouth in what appeared to be a smile, as though he approved of their new names. Some of the raisins dropped out of his mouth, and quickly one of the babies picked them up.

"Nothing goes to waste in this raccoon family," said Jerri's mother.

★ 5 ★

Star and the Baby Lamb

Star's name for Jerri's pet lamb was "Bootie." This made Jerri laugh every time she said it. "Not 'Bootie,' Star," he would say, " 'Beauty.' Booties are something you wear in the wintertime, when it snows."

"I know," said Star. "You call her 'Bootie' because she is bootiful!"

"That's right," Jerri told her. "She's a beautiful lamb."

"I wish she were mine," Star said.

"Well," Jerri began, "tomorrow I have to go with my mother into the city. We're going to the dentist so that when I grow up I'll have beautiful teeth just like my father's. You can have Beauty all day tomorrow," Jerri told Star, "and make believe that she is your own pet lamb."

"Oh," exclaimed Star, "can I really have Bootie for a whole day and make believe she is mine? Really mine?"

"That's right," said Jerri. "But you have to give her back to me when I come home."

"Oh, I'll have fun with Bootie," said Star. "When I take my nap, I'll make her take one, too. I'll make her lie down right beside me."

"Look, Star," said Jerri, "Beauty isn't a playmate. She's just a little lamb. Maybe she won't want to lie down."

"I'll make her," said Star. "We'll have fun. I'll make her do all kinds of things."

Jerri laughed. "Well, don't try to make her sit up like a dog," he said. " 'Cause no lamb can sit up like a dog."

"Okay," said Star. "Even though Bootie can't sit up like a dog, we'll have fun."

The following morning, Jerri brought Beauty over to Star's house. Star was delighted when she saw the little lamb.

"Oh, Grammy," she said, "Bootie's going to stay the whole day with me. I'm going to make believe that she's really my lamb. You see, Grammy, Jerri's mother is taking him to the city to get him some bootiful teeth. When Jerri comes home, he's going to have teeth just like his daddy's."

Star's grandmother laughed. "So Jerri is going to have beautiful teeth like his father's?"

"That's right," said Star. "He told me all about it."

The first thing Star did with the little lamb was to put the pink sash from her dress around its neck. "Now Bootie is bootiful," she said.

Star spent most of the morning running after the lamb and patting it. Late in the morning, Star spied a baby bottle on a shelf in the kitchen. "Oh, Grammy," she cried, pointing to the bottle, "there's a baby bottle up on that shelf."

"That's right," said her grandmother. "I guess we're hoping that someday there'll be another baby around here."

"Well," said Star, "if you would put some milk in that bottle, I could feed Bootie and make believe she's a baby."

"I'll do that," said her grandmother. "It's almost lunchtime."

Star's grandmother took the bottle off the shelf and filled it with warm milk. There was still a nipple on the bottle, and when Star put it against Beauty's mouth, she opened it and took hold of the nipple and began to suck.

Star laughed with delight as the little lamb drank the milk. "Oh, Grammy," she cried, "I'm having such fun with Bootie."

"Well, I'm glad you're enjoying yourself," said her grandmother. She placed a bowl of soup on the kitchen table. "Now," she said, "come and have your lunch out of a bowl and not out of a bottle."

Star sat down at the table and began to eat her soup. "Oh, Grammy," she said, "I didn't know it would be so much fun. Now Bootie's my baby. She takes her milk just like a baby. I'll have to see what else my baby would like."

After lunch, Star picked up her doll and went outdoors. The doll had on a beautiful pink bonnet and pink cape. Star removed the bonnet and the cape and said, "Now I'll have to see how my baby looks in a bonnet." Star took hold of the lamb. With great difficulty, she put the bonnet on the lamb's head. When she saw its little face looking out of the bonnet, she clapped her hands with delight. Then she picked up the pink cape and put it around the lamb's back. This delighted her even more. "Oh, Grammy," she cried, pulling

Beauty into the house, "just look at my bootiful baby!"

Her grandmother laughed and said, "I don't think that lamb is going to stay in that bonnet and cape for very long."

When it came time for Star's nap, she tried very hard to get the lamb onto her bed, but the lamb kept pulling away. So Star took her nap while Beauty wiggled out of the bonnet and the cape.

When Star woke up, she put the bonnet and cape back on the lamb. But they didn't stay on for very long. Beauty didn't seem to like her clothes, and so she wiggled out of them again and again. But Star was not discouraged. She kept gathering up the bonnet and cape and putting them back on the little lamb.

At the end of the day, when Jerri came to get Beauty, he was amazed to see her wearing a pink bonnet and a pink cape. "Oh, Star," he cried, "what have you done to Beauty?"

Star stood proudly admiring the little lamb. "Isn't she bootiful?" Star said.

"She looks crazy," said Jerri. "I don't like my lamb looking like a doll baby."

"Oh, she's bootiful," said Star. "She's been my baby all day."

⋆ 6 ⋆

More News About the Swans

There was great excitement over the nesting swans. Mr. Sawyer had counted eight eggs in the nest, and the swans were taking turns sitting on them. Because the swans looked exactly alike to the children, Star and Jerri never knew whether it was the mama swan or the papa swan who was sitting on the eggs. But they both seemed very faithful to the nest.

One morning, Star said to her grandfather, "Grampy, I want to go and see the swannies."

"Well, you mustn't get too close to them, especially when they're nesting," her grandfather told her. "But I'll take you over for a peek."

Star took hold of her grandfather's hand, and they crossed the road. Suddenly Star called out, "Oh, Grampy, look! One of the eggs has rolled out of the nest."

"Why, so it has," said her grandfather.

"You'll have to put the egg back in the nest," said Star. "I wonder if the swannies count the eggs and know that one is missing."

"I don't know," said her grandfather, "if swans can count."

"Well, quick, Grampy, put the egg back," said Star.

"I'm not going to put the egg back," said her grandfather. "I'm not going to go near that swan."

"Why, Grampy, are you afraid of the swannie?" asked Star.

"I don't want that swan to take a bite out of me," said her grandfather. "She'd probably like to taste me, but I won't let her."

"Why, Grampy," exclaimed Star, "I didn't know that grampies were ever afraid."

"Well, sometimes they are," said her grandfather.

"And are grammies ever afraid?" asked Star.

"I guess sometimes grammies are afraid, too," replied her grandfather.

"Oh." Star was quiet for a while. "I thought only children were afraid," she said.

"Well, now you've found out a secret." Her grandfather smiled.

Star let out a little squeal and said, "I know a secret." And she looked up at her grandfather. "But I won't tell."

"That's good," he said. "Because we don't want everybody to know that grampies and grammies can get scared."

Star watched her grandfather as he tiptoed over to the egg. She watched him take a large handkerchief from his pocket and carefully fold the egg within it. He tied a knot so that he was able to carry the egg carefully. Then he picked it up gently.

"Now what are we going to do with this egg?" Star asked. "Maybe I could sit on it. I could keep it warm until the baby swannie comes out."

"No," said her grandfather, "you couldn't sit on it."

"Maybe we could put it in the oven," said Star. "We could keep it warm there."

"No, we wouldn't know what temperature to have in the oven," said her grandfather. "Now I have to think fast, because we can't keep this egg out of the nest too long."

"Oh, yes, Grampy," said Star. "Think fast!"

In a moment her grandfather said, "I know what to do! My friend Jim Walters, over on Route 85, has a large pond. This time of the year, a flock of

Canada geese settle there for a short time. Two of them always make a nest. I think Jim probably has Canada geese now because I've seen some flying overhead. We'll take this egg over to Jim and see if he will put it in that nest."

"Oh, Grampy," cried Star, "that's a wonderful idea! But won't your friend be afraid of the Canada geese?"

"I don't think so," said her grandfather. "They are more friendly than your swannies. Come, we'll drive right over to Jim's place."

Just then Jerri appeared. Star told him about the egg rolling out of the nest. "Grampy and I are going to take it over to Mr. Walters," said Star. "He'll put it into a nest so that a bird can sit on it until the baby swannie hatches out."

"What kind of bird?" asked Jerri.

"Canada geese," said Grampy.

"Can I come with you?" asked Jerri. "I'd like to see the Canada geese."

"Come along," said Grandfather. "We're going right now."

Soon their grandfather had backed his car out of the garage and the children climbed in beside him.

33

"I want to carry the egg," said Star. "This egg has a baby swannie inside of it."

"It's called a cygnet," said Jerri, with a very important air.

"I know," said Star. "Aunt Jessie told me."

"Well, don't drop it," said their grandfather, "or there won't be any cygnet at all."

On the way, Jerri said, "I've seen Canada geese flying overhead for some time. I guess they were on the way to Mr. Walters's place. Funny, they don't ever come down to where the swans are."

Grampy laughed. "I guess they're choosy and like the water better over at Jim's pond. I just hope the Canada geese will accept this egg."

It wasn't long before Grampy drove into Mr. Walters's driveway. They found him out near the pond looking at the Canada geese swimming in the water. Grampy called "Hello" to his friend and said, "Aren't they a beautiful sight? Do you have a couple nesting?"

Mr. Walters nodded and smiled at the children.

"Well," said Grampy, "you know my grandchildren, Star and Jerri. We've come over with a surprise for those Canada geese. Two swans are nesting on Sawyer's pond and we've brought an egg that fell out of the nest. Do you think your Canada geese would keep this swan's egg warm until the cygnet hatches out?"

"Well, we can try," said Mr. Walters. "I wouldn't know, and as I don't speak their language, I can't ask the Canada geese! Let me have the egg, and I'll do the best I can."

Grampy handed the egg to his friend and said, "I hope you can sneak it in on them."

Mr. Walters took the egg and started to walk to the nest. "You'd better all stay right here because these Canada geese don't like too much company while they're nesting."

Grandfather and the children watched Mr. Walters as he went off with the egg. "He won't drop it, will he?" said Star to her grandfather.

"I'm sure he won't," said her grandfather. "He'll be very careful."

Now Mr. Walters was too far away for the children to see him. But when he returned, he said, "I slipped it in. I hope in about a month I'll be able to report that the cygnet has hatched out. I'll let you know when it arrives."

"Oh, thank you," said Star. "I can't wait to see the baby swannie."

Now Star told everyone that she met, "We're

going to have a baby." She told the postal worker at the post office, the man who kept the grocery store, and everyone who came to see her grandmother.

Then Star would say, "We took the egg to Mr. Walters's place 'cause he has Canada geese nesting. The baby is going to be born in their nest."

Everyone was relieved to know that the "baby" was going to be a small bird called a cygnet. Now everyone was asking Star, "Has the baby come yet?"

"Not yet, but soon," Star would reply.

7

The Raccoon's Surprise

One evening, Grammy said to Star, "Would you like to go down and have a little visit with Jerri before you go to bed?"

"Oh, yes," said Star. "And maybe the raccoons will come."

Star and her grandmother crossed the road and went down to Jerri's house. Aunt Jessie welcomed them at the front door, and Jerri came running, glad to see Star.

"Oh, Star," he said, "come on into the dining room. I'm working on a jigsaw puzzle. You can help me."

"Well," said Aunt Jessie to Grammy, "come sit with me in the parlor. I was just about to make an apple pie when you knocked. I can stop now a bit and put the baking off for a while."

Star ran to the dining room. She climbed onto a chair to look at the jigsaw puzzle that Jerri was making. Jerri sat down and said, "This is a wonderful puzzle, Star. There are horses in it, and you know I like pictures with horses in them."

"I like horses, too," said Star. "And I can see that all the pieces of white will help to make a white horse."

"That's right," said Jerri.

Just then there was the sound of the back screen door closing. Star looked up at Jerri. He said, "I guess that's Daddy. He's probably going to have a cup of coffee."

Now there was a mysterious little thumping sound. Jerri said, "I wonder what else Daddy's up to. Maybe he's going to have a cookie."

Soon there was a scraping sound. Jerri said, "Let's go see what Daddy's doing."

Jerri and Star went out to the kitchen and stared in amazement. Instead of Jerri's daddy, there were George and Mildred and their babies scrambling around. One of the grown-up raccoons was up on the table and had knocked a bag of flour onto the floor. The bag had split open, and flour was flying all over the room.

"Oh, Mother!" Jerri called as he ran toward the parlor. "Come quick! Come quick! The raccoons are in the kitchen!"

"Oh, where's Star?" Grammy cried out as they all headed for the kitchen.

"She's in the kitchen with the raccoons," said Jerri.

"Oh, dear," Grammy cried. "I hope she hasn't touched them. I hope she remembers I've told her never to touch wild animals."

Now they had reached the kitchen and found that Star had been dusted by flying flour. She was standing beside the kitchen table, looking delighted at what she saw. The raccoons were rolling in the flour, having a wonderful time.

"Land o' mercy!" cried Aunt Jessie. "Look at this mess the raccoons have made. I just took that flour out of the cupboard."

The children were laughing very hard and were enjoying this unexpected performance.

"Aren't they naughty little raccoons?" said Star.

"Oh, they're just having fun," said Jerri.

"Yes," said Star. "I think they're the cutest things I've ever seen."

"Not so cute to me!" said Aunt Jessie as she held the screen door open and used the broom to shoo them out the back door.

"Oh, don't hurt them," cried Star. "Don't hurt them!"

"I'm not hurting them," said Aunt Jessie. "This will just help to get the flour off them. Those little ones look more like baby skunks than baby raccoons."

Taking the broom, Jerri said, "Here, Mother, I'll help clean up the kitchen."

"I'm glad they've gone," said Jerri's mother. "They don't belong in the house."

"Oh, I wish they would come to visit us," said Star.

Grammy held up her hands and cried, "I'm not going to invite them into our house!"

"But, Grammy," said Star, "they are so cute. Don't you think they're cute?"

"Well, I might think they're cute if they stay outdoors where raccoons belong," said her grandmother.

"I'll agree with that," said Aunt Jessie. "Now, when I get everything cleaned up, I'll make the apple pie. And I'll make an extra, a nice little pie we can eat right away. And we'll save a piece for Uncle Jess, too."

"Oh, goody!" said Jerri. "I wish Daddy could

have seen those raccoons."

"You can tell him that his friend Mildred came in and knocked the bag of flour on the floor."

"I think Daddy would have laughed," said Jerri.

"Well," said Jerri's mother, "if those raccoons want more raisins, they had better behave themselves and stay out of my kitchen."

★ *8* ★

The Birthday

Star was on tiptoes with excitement as she waited for the arrival of the cygnet. Every day she asked her grandfather, "Do you think Mr. Walters will telephone today and tell us that our baby has arrived?"

"When the day comes, Star," said her grandfather, "I know he'll tell us. You just be patient and stop jumping up and down."

At last the morning came when the telephone rang and Star's grandfather picked up the receiver. Star was right at his elbow, saying, "Is it him, Grampy? Is it him?"

When her grandfather hung up, he said, "Yes, Star, the cygnet was born this morning. Jim says it is already swimming with the Canada geese.

Some of their eggs hatched out, and they already seem like a happy family."

"Oh, Grampy," said Star, "when can we go over and get our baby? Can we go right now?"

"You'll have to give me time to find a nice carton to carry this little bird in," said her grandfather. "So as soon as I find a carton we can go."

It didn't take her grandfather very long to find a carton suitable for carrying the bird. In the meantime, Jerri arrived.

"Isn't it 'citing, Jerri?" said Star. "Now we can go to get the baby."

"Star," said Jerri, "you mean *exciting*. It's time for you to grow up and stop using baby talk. It's not 'citing. It's *exciting*!"

"It's very *exciting*," said Star. "I can hardly wait to see that baby swannie, that *beautiful* little white swannie with his little yellow beak."

Now their grandfather was ready to leave. "Come along," he said. "Let's go get this bird."

The children climbed into the car beside their grandfather, and he started off for Jim Walters's place.

As soon as they arrived, the children jumped down and ran to the big pond. They stood on the

44

edge and saw the Canada geese swimming in the water followed by several little ones.

"Oh," cried Star, "which one is our baby? Which one? I don't see any little white one."

"Oh, cygnets are not white when they're born," said Mr. Walters. "They're tawny little things. You can see some of the baby Canada geese. They're very fluffy and gray. And they are a bit smaller than your cygnet."

Star was jumping up and down with excitement. She pointed to the cygnet and cried, "Oh, it isn't white like the other swannies. I thought the baby would look just like them."

"Well, you'll have to wait awhile," said Grampy. "Just wait until it grows up, and then it will look like its mom and pop. You're in too great a hurry, Star."

"Well, anyway, the baby's here," said Star. "And now we'll have to have a birthday party."

"Star," said Jerri, "you can't have a birthday party because you don't have a number."

"What do you mean, a number?" asked Star. "I don't understand."

"Well, how old are you?" asked Jerri.

"I'm five," Star answered.

"See," said Jerri, "you've got a number. I'm seven, so I have a number, too. But that little cygnet was just born. It doesn't have a number yet. When you have a number, then you can have candles on a birthday cake. This cygnet won't have a candle. See what I mean, Star?"

"Well, I don't care," said Star. "We're going to have a birthday party."

"I suppose you're going to invite the raccoons to the party," said Jerri.

"Oh, no," said Star. "That wouldn't be a nice party. You know swannies don't like raccoons. But we'll give the raccoons some crumbs from the birthday cake. We can put the crumbs on the back step. We'll give the baby and the big swannies some of the birthday cake. We'll throw it right into the water for them."

"Well," said Jerri, "I hope my piece of birthday cake won't be floating on water."

Star laughed and said, "No, Jerri, your piece of birthday cake will be yummy."

"I'm glad," said Jerri. "Now, what are you going to name this baby swannie?"

"I think it would be nice to name it 'Jessie,' " said Star. "Then it would be named after both

Aunt Jessie and Uncle Jess."

"Oh," said Jerri, "I think they'll be very pleased. They'll think it's a great honor. And they would like some of that birthday cake, too. But I've never seen a birthday cake without a candle. There's nothing to blow out."

"Don't worry about that," said Grampy. "Grammy will probably put a sparkler on the cake. You know, the sparklers we have on Fourth of July. It will be much prettier than just candles."

"Oh, yes," cried Star, "much prettier!"

"Before you talk anymore about a birthday party," said Grampy, "we've got to get this little bird to our pond and see what kind of welcome it gets from those two big swans. Let's get this little cygnet into the carton."

"I think I can manage that," said Mr. Walters. "I have some corn in my pocket. I think the cygnet will accept it." Mr. Walters kneeled down beside the pond and held out his hand with the corn to the birds. The cygnet soon swam over, and he was able to pick it up and place it inside the carton.

"You're a real birdman, Jim," said the children's grandfather.

"Just takes a little know-how," said Mr. Walters. "And by the way, I've saved some pieces of the egg from which this bird was hatched. They're so pretty, I thought you'd like to keep them."

Mr. Walters went into the house and came back with some pieces of the large egg.

"Oh," Jerri said. "I thought it would be a pretty color."

Grampy winked at Mr. Walters. "I guess you thought it would be red, white, and blue," he said.

Jerry laughed. "That's all right," he told Mr. Walters. "I'll keep my piece till school begins. Then I can take it for Show and Tell. I bet no one else will bring part of a swan's egg. I'll tell the kids all about this little cygnet."

The children's grandfather put the carton in the car, and in a few minutes Grampy and the children were on their way home.

When they arrived at their pond, they found the two swans swimming around in the water, followed by seven little cygnets, for the eggs that they had been keeping warm had hatched. While Star and Jerri watched, their grandfather opened the carton. Jessie jumped out and headed right for the water. Star and Jerri held their breath, won-

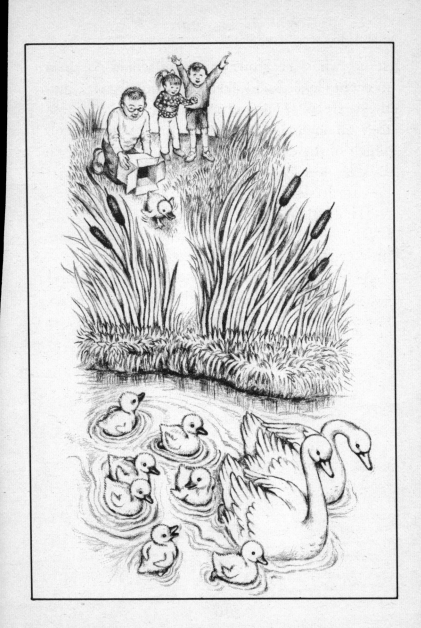

dering what the grown-up swans would do. In a moment, Jessie had joined the other cygnets, and they were all swimming around the pond. Because they all looked alike, the children couldn't tell which of the cygnets was Jessie.

"Oh, dear," cried Star, "all of those little babies are Jessies!"

"That's right," said Jerri. "I think Mother and Daddy will be glad to know that there are so many little cygnets named after them."

As Star watched the cygnets swimming behind the big swans, she couldn't tell which one was her Jessie. But she loved them all.